Nennius

History of the Britons (Historia Brittonum)

in large print

Nennius

History of the Britons (Historia Brittonum)

in large print

Reproduction of the original.

1st Edition 2023 | ISBN: 978-3-38701-587-4

Megali Verlag is an imprint of Outlook Verlagsgesellschaft mbH.

Verlag (Publisher): Outlook Verlag GmbH, Zeilweg 44, 60439 Frankfurt, Deutschland
Vertretungsberechtigt (Authorized to represent): E. Roepke, Zeilweg 44, 60439 Frankfurt, Deutschland
Druck (Print): Books on Demand GmbH, In de Tarpen 42, 22848 Norderstedt, Deutschland

HISTORY OF THE BRITONS

(HISTORIA BRITTONUM)

by Nennius

Translated by J. A. Giles

I. THE PROLOGUE.

1. Nennius, the lowly minister and servant of the servants of God, by the grace of God, disciple of St. Elbotus,* to all the followers of truth sendeth health.

* Or Elvod, bishop of Bangor, A.D. 755, who first adopted in the Cambrian church the new cycle for regulating Easter.

Be it known to your charity, that being dull in intellect and rude of speech, I have presumed to deliver these things in the Latin tongue, not trusting to my own learning, which is little or none at all, but partly from traditions of our ancestors, partly from writings and monuments of the ancient inhabitants of Britain, partly from the annals of the Romans, and the chronicles of the sacred fathers, Isidore, Hieronymus, Prosper, Eusebius, and from the histories of the Scots and Saxons, although our enemies, not following my own inclinations, but, to the best of my ability, obeying the commands of my seniors; I have lispingly put together this history from various sources, and have endeavored, from shame, to deliver down to posterity the few remaining ears of corn about past transactions, that they might not be trodden under foot, seeing that an ample crop has been snatched away already by the hostile reapers of foreign nations. For many things have been in my way, and I, to this day, have hardly been able to understand, even superficially, as was necessary, the sayings of other men; much less was I able in my own strength, but like a barbarian, have I murdered and defiled the language of others. But I bore about with me an inward wound, and I was indignant, that the name of my own people, formerly famous and distinguished, should sink into oblivion, and like smoke be dissipated. But since, however, I had rather myself be the historian of the Britons than nobody, although so many are to be found who might much more satisfactorily discharge the labour thus imposed on me; I humbly entreat my readers, whose ears I may offend by the inelegance of my words, that they will fulfil the wish of my seniors, and grant me the easy task of listening with candour to my history. For zealous efforts very often fail: but bold enthusiasm, were it in its power, would not suffer me to fail. May, therefore, candour be shown where the inelegance of my words is insufficient, and may the truth of this history, which my rustic tongue has ventured, as a kind of plough, to trace out in furrows, lose none of its influence from that cause, in the ears of my hearers. For it is better to drink a wholesome draught of truth from the humble vessel, than poison mixed with honey from a golden goblet.

2. And do not be loath, diligent reader, to winnow my chaff, and lay up the wheat in the storehouse of your memory: for truth regards not who is the speaker, nor in what manner it is spoken, but that the thing be true; and she does not despise the jewel which she has rescued from the mud, but she adds it to her former treasures.

For I yield to those who are greater and more eloquent than myself, who, kindled with generous ardour, have endeavoured by Roman eloquence to smooth the jarring elements of their tongue, if they have left unshaken any pillar of history which I wished to see remain. This history therefore has been compiled from a wish to benefit my inferiors, not from envy of those who are superior to me, in the 858th year of our Lord's incarnation, and in the 24th year of Mervin, king of the Britons, and I hope that the prayers of my betters will be offered up for me in recompence of my labour. But this is sufficient by way of preface. I shall obediently accomplish the rest to the utmost of my power.

II. THE APOLOGY OF NENNIUS

Here begins the apology of Nennius, the historiographer of the Britons, of the race of the Britons.

3. I, Nennius, disciple of St. Elbotus, have endeavoured to write some extracts which the dulness of the British nation had cast away, because teachers had no knowledge, nor gave any information in their books about this island of Britain. But I have got together all that I could find as well from the annals of the Romans as from the chronicles of the sacred fathers, Hieronymus, Eusebius, Isidorus, Prosper, and from the annals of the Scots and Saxons, and from our ancient traditions. Many teachers and scribes have attempted to write this, but somehow or other have abandoned it from its difficulty, either on account of frequent deaths, or the often recurring calamities of war. I pray that every reader who shall read this book, may pardon me, for having attempted, like a chattering jay, or like some weak witness, to write

these things, after they had failed. I yield to him who knows more of these things than I do.

III. THE HISTORY.

4, 5. From Adam to the flood, are two thousand and forty-two years. From the flood of Abraham, nine hundred and forty-two. From Abraham to Moses, six hundred.* From Moses to Solomon, and the first building of the temple, four hundred and forty-eight. From Solomon to the rebuilding of the temple, which was under Darius, king of the Persians, six hundred and twelve years are computed. From Darius to the ministry of our Lord Jesus Christ, and to the fifteenth year of the emperor Tiberius, are five hundred and forty-eight years. So that from Adam to the ministry of Christ and the fifteenth year of the emperor Tiberius, are five thousand two hundred and twenty-eight years. From the passion of Christ are completed nine hundred and forty-six; from his incarnation, nine hundred and seventy-six: being the fifth year of Edmund, king of the Angles.

* And forty, according to Stevenson's new edition. The rest of this chronology is much contracted in several of the manuscripts, and hardly two of them contain it exactly the same.

6. The first age of the world is from Adam to Noah; the second from Noah to Abraham; the third from Abraham to David; the fourth from David to Daniel; the fifth to John the

Baptist; the sixth from John to the judgment, when our Lord Jesus Christ will come to judge the living and the dead, and the world by fire.

The first Julius.
The second Claudius.
The third Severus.
The fourth Carinus.
The fifth Constantius.
The sixth Maximus.
The seventh Maximianus.
The eighth another Severus Aequantius.
The ninth Constantius.*

* This list of the Roman emperors who visited Britain, is omitted in many of the MSS.

Here beginneth the history of the Britons, edited by Mark the anchorite, a holy bishop of that people.

7. The island of Britain derives its name from Brutus, a Roman consul. Taken from the south-west point it inclines a little towards the west, and to its northern extremity measures eight hundred miles, and is in breadth two hundred. It contains thirty three cities,(1) viz.

1. Cair ebrauc (York).
2. Cair ceint (Canterbury).
3. Cair gurcoc (Anglesey?).
4. Cair guorthegern (2)
5. Cair custeint (Carnarvon).
6. Cair guoranegon (Worcester).
7. Cair segeint (Silchester).
8. Cair guin truis (Norwich, or Winwick).

9. Cair merdin (Caermarthen).
10. Cair peris (Porchester).
11. Cair lion (Caerleon-upon-Usk).
12. Cair mencipit (Verulam).
13. Cair caratauc (Catterick).
14. Cair ceri (Cirencester).
15. Cair glout (Gloucester).
16. Cair luillid (Carlisle).
17. Cair grant (Grantchester, now Cambridge).
18. Cair daun (Doncaster), or Cair dauri (Dorchester).
19. Cair britoc (Bristol).
20. Cair meguaid (Meivod).
21. Cair mauiguid (Manchester).
22. Cair ligion (Chester).
23. Cair guent (Winchester, or Caerwent, in Monmouthshire).
24. Cair collon (Colchester, or St. Colon, Cornwall).
25. Cair londein (London).
26. Cair guorcon (Worren, or Woran, in Pembrokeshire).
27. Cair lerion (Leicester).
28. Cair draithou (Drayton).
29. Cair pensavelcoit (Pevensey, in Sussex).
30. Cairtelm (Teyn-Grace, in Devonshire).
31. Cair Urnahc (Wroxeter, in Shropshire).
32. Cair colemion (Camelet, in Somersetshire).
33. Cair loit coit (Lincoln).
(1) V.R. Twenty-eight, twenty-one.
(2) Site unknown.

These are the names of the ancient cities of the island of Britain. It has also a vast many promontories, and castles innumerable, built of brick and stone. Its inhabitants consist of four different people; the Scots, the Picts, the Saxons and the ancient Britons.

8. Three considerable islands belong to it; one, on the south, opposite the Armorican shore, called Wight;* another between Ireland and Britain, called Eubonia or Man; and another directly north, beyond the Picts, named Orkney; and hence it was anciently a proverbial expression, in reference to its kings and rulers, "He reigned over Britain and its three islands."

* Inis-gueith, or Gueith.

6. It is fertilized by several rivers, which traverse it in all directions, to the east and west, to the south and north; but there are two pre-eminently distinguished among the rest, the Thames and the Severn, which formerly, like the two arms of Britain, bore the ships employed in the conveyance of riches acquired by commerce. The Britons were once very populous, and exercised extensive dominion from sea to sea.

10.* Respecting the period when this island became inhabited subsequently to the flood, I have seen two distinct relations. According to the annals of the Roman history, the Britons deduce their origin both from the Greeks and Romans. On the side of the mother, from Lavinia, the daughter of Latinus, king of Italy, and of the race of Silvanus, the son of Inachus, the son of Dardanus; who was the son of Saturn, king of the Greeks, and who, having possessed himself of a part of Asia, built the city of Troy. Dardanus was the father of Troius, who was the father of Priam and Anchises; Anchises was the father of Aeneas, who was the father of Ascanius and Silvius; and this Silvius was the son of Aeneas and Lavinia, the daughter of the king of Italy. From the sons of Aeneas and Lavinia descended Romulus and Remus, who were the sons of the holy queen Rhea, and the founders of Rome. Brutus was consul when he conquered Spain, and reduced that country to a Roman province. He afterwards subdued the island of Britain, whose inhabitants were the descendants of the Romans, from Silvius Posthumus. He was called Posthumus because he was born after the death of Aeneas his father; and his mother Lavinia concealed herself during her pregnancy; he was called Silvius, because he was born in a wood. Hence the Roman kings were called Silvan, and the Britons from Brutus, and rose from the family of Brutus.

* The whole of this, as far as the end of the paragraph, is omitted in several MSS.

Aeneas, after the Trojan war, arrived with his son in Italy; and Having vanquished Turnus, married Lavinia, the daughter of king Latinus, who was the son of Faunus, the son of Picus, the son of Saturn. After the death of Latinus, Aeneas obtained the kingdom Of the Romans, and Lavinia brought forth a son, who was named Silvius. Ascanius founded Alba, and afterwards married. And Lavinia bore to Aeneas a son, named Silvius; but Ascanius (1) married a wife, who conceived and became pregnant. And Aeneas, having been informed that his daughter-in-law was pregnant, ordered his son to send his magician to examine his wife, whether the child conceived were male or female. The magician came and examined the wife and pronounced it to be a son, who should become the most valiant among the Italians, and the most beloved of all men. (2) In consequence of this prediction, the magician was put to death by Ascanius; but it happened that the mother of the child dying at its birth, he was named Brutus; ad after a certain interval, agreeably to what the magician had foretold, whilst he was playing with some others he shot his father with an arrow, not intentionally but by accident. (3) He was, for this cause, expelled from Italy, and came to the islands of the Tyrrhene sea, when he was exiled on account of the death of Turnus, slain by Aeneas. He then went among the Gauls, and built the city of the Turones, called Turnis. (4) At length he came to this island named from him Britannia, dwelt there, and filled it with his own descendants, and it has been inhabited from that time to the present period.

(1) Other MSS. Silvius.

(2) V.R. Who should slay his father and mother, and be hated
by all mankind.

(3) V.R. He displayed such superiority among his play-fellows, that they seemed to consider him as their chief.

(4) Tours.

11. Aeneas reigned over the Latins three years; Ascanius thirty three years; after whom Silvius reigned twelve years,

and Posthumus thirty-nine * years: the latter, from whom the kings of Alba are called Silvan, was brother to Brutus, who governed Britain at the time Eli the high-priest judged Israel, and when the ark of the covenant was taken by a foreign people. But Posthumus his brother reigned among the Latins. * V.R. Thirty-seven.

12. After an interval of not less than eight hundred years, came the Picts, and occupied the Orkney Islands: whence they laid waste many regions, and seized those on the left hand side of Britain, where they still remain, keeping possession of a third part of Britain to this day. *
* See Bede's Eccles. Hist.

13. Long after this, the Scots arrived in Ireland from Spain. The first that came was Partholomus,(1) with a thousand men and women; these increased to four thousand; but a mortality coming suddenly upon them, they all perished in one week. The second was Nimech, the son of...,(2) who, according to report, after having been at sea a year and a half, and having his ships shattered, arrived at a port in Ireland, and continuing there several years, returned at length with his followers to Spain. After these came three sons of a Spanish soldier with thirty ships, each of which contained thirty wives; and having remained there during the space of a year, there appeared to them, in the middle of the sea, a tower of glass, the summit of which seemed covered with men, to whom they often spoke, but received no answer. At length they determined to besiege the tower; and after a year's preparation, advanced towards it, with the whole number of their ships, and all the women, one ship

only excepted, which had been wrecked, and in which were thirty men, and as many women; but when all had disembarked on the shore which surrounded the tower, the sea opened and swallowed them up. Ireland, however, was peopled, to the present period, from the family remaining in the vessel which was wrecked. Afterwards, other came from Spain, and possessed themselves of various parts of Britain.

(1) V.R. Partholomaeus, or Bartholomaeus.

(2) A blank is here in the MS. Agnomen is found in some of the others.

14. Last of all came one Hoctor,(1) who continued there, and whose descendants remain there to this day. Istoreth, the son of Istorinus, with his followers, held Dalrieta; Buile had the island Eubonia, and other adjacent places. The sons of Liethali(2) obtained the country of the dimetae, where is a city called Menavia,(3) and the province Guiher and Cetgueli, (4) which they held till they were expelled from every part of Britain, by Cunedda and his sons.

(1) V.R. Damhoctor, Clamhoctor, and Elamhoctor.

(2) V.R. Liethan, Bethan, Vethan.

(3) St. David's.

(4) Guiher, probably the Welsh district Gower. Cetgueli is Caer Kidwelly, in Carmarthenshire.

15. According to the most learned among the Scots, if any one desires to learn what I am now going to state, Ireland

was a desert, and uninhabited, when the children of Israel crossed the Red Sea, in which, as we read in the Book of the Law, the Egyptians who followed them were drowned. At that period, there lived among this people, with a numerous family, a Scythian of noble birth, who had been banished from his country and did not go to pursue the people of God. The Egyptians who were left, seeing the destruction of the great men of their nation, and fearing lest he should possess himself of their territory, took counsel together, and expelled him. Thus reduced, he wandered forty-two years in Africa, and arrived, with his family, at the altars of the Philistines, by the Lake of Osiers. Then passing between Rusicada and the hilly country of Syria, they travelled by the river Malva through Mauritania as far as the Pillars of Hercules; and crossing the Tyrrhene Sea, landed in Spain, where they continued many years, having greatly increased and multiplied. Thence, a thousand and two years after the Egyptians were lost in the Red Sea, they passed into Ireland, and the district of Dalrieta.* At that period, Brutus, who first exercised the consular office, reigned over the Romans; and the state, which before was governed by regal power, was afterwards ruled, during four hundred and forty-seven years, by consuls, tribunes of the people, and dictators.

* North-western part of Antrim in Ulster.

The Britons came to Britain in the third age of the world; and in the fourth, the Scots took possession of Ireland.

The Britons who, suspecting no hostilities, were unprovided with the means of defence, were unanimously and incessantly attacked, both by the Scots from the west, and by the Picts from the north. A long interval after this, the Romans obtained the empire of the world.

16. From the first arrival of the Saxons into Britain, to the fourth year of king Mermenus, are computed four hundred and twenty eight years; from the nativity of our Lord to the coming of St. Patrick among the Scots, four hundred and five years; from the death of St. Patrick to that of St. Bridget, forty years; and from the birth of Columeille(1) to the death of St Bridget four years.(2)

(1) V.R. Columba.

(2) Some MSS. add, the beginning of the calculation is 23 cycles of 19 years from the incarnation of our Lord to the arrival of St. Patrick in Ireland, and they make 438 years. And from the arrival of St. Patrick to the cycle of 19 years in which we live are 22 cycles, which make 421 years.

17. I have learned another account of this Brutus from the ancient books of our ancestors.* After the deluge, the three sons of Noah severally occupied three different parts of the earth: Shem extended his borders into Asia, Ham into Africa, and Japheth in Europe.

* This proves the tradition of Brutus to be older than Geoffrey or Tyssilio, unless these notices of Brutus have been interpolated in the original work of Nennius.

The first man that dwelt in Europe was Alanus, with his three sons, Hisicion, Armenon, and Neugio. Hisicion had four sons, Francus, Romanus, Alamanus, and Brutus. Armenon had five sons, Gothus, Valagothus, Cibidus, Burgundus, and Longobardus. Neugio had three sons, Vandalus, Saxo, and

Boganus. From Hisicion arose four nations—the Franks, the Latins, the Germans, and Britons: from Armenon, the Gothi, Balagothi, Cibidi, Burgundi, and Longobardi: from Neugio, the Bogari, Vandali, Saxones, and Tarinegi. The whole of Europe was subdivided into these tribes.

Alanus is said to have been the son of Fethuir;* Fethuir, the son of Ogomuin, who was the son of Thoi; Thoi was the son of Boibus, Boibus of Semion, Semion of Mair, Mair of Ecthactus, Ecthactus of Aurthack, Aurthack of Ethec, Ethec of Ooth, Ooth of Aber, Aber of Ra, Ra of Esraa, Esraa of Hisrau, Hisrau of Bath, Bath of Jobath, Jobath of Joham, Joham of Japheth, Japheth of Noah, Noah of Lamech, Lamech of Mathusalem, Mathusalem of Enoch, Enoch of Jared, Jared of Malalehel, Malalehel of Cainan, Cainan of Enos, Enos of Seth, Seth of Adam, and Adam was formed by the living God. We have obtained this information respecting the original inhabitants of Britain from ancient tradition.

* This genealogy is different in almost all the MSS.

18. The Britons were thus called from Brutus: Brutus was the son of Hisicion, Hisicion was the son of Alanus, Alanus was the son of Rhea Silvia, Fhea Silvia was the daughter of Numa Pompilius, Numa was the son of Ascanius, Ascanius of Eneas, Eneas of Anchises, Anchises of Troius, Troius of Dardanus, Dardanus of Flisa, Flisa of Juuin, Juuin of Japheth; but Japheth had seven sons; from the first named Gomer, descended the Galli; from the second, Magog, the Scythi and Gothi; from the third, Madian, the Medi; from the fourth, Juuan, the Greeks; from the fifth, Tubal, arose the Hebrei, Hispani, and Itali; from the sixth, Mosoch, sprung the

Cappadoces; and from the seventh, named Tiras, descended the Thraces: these are the sons of Japheth, the son of Noah, the son of Lamech.

19.* The Romans, having obtained the dominion of the world, sent legates or deputies to the Britons to demand of them hostages and tribute, which they received from all other countries and islands; but they, fierce, disdainful, and haughty, treated the legation with contempt.

* Some MSS. add, I will now return to the point from which I made this digression.

Then Julius Caesar, the first who had acquired absolute power at Rome, highly incensed against the Britons, sailed with sixty vessels to the mouth of the Thames, where they suffered shipwreck whilst he fought against Dolobellus, (the proconsul of the British king, who was called Belinus, and who was the son of Minocannus who governed all the islands of the Tyrrhene Sea), and thus Julius Caesar returned home without victory, having had his soldiers Slain, and his ships shattered.

20. But after three years he again appeared with a large army, and three hundred ships, at the mouth of the Thames, where he renewed hostilities. In this attempt many of his soldiers and horses were killed; for the same consul had placed iron pikes in the shallow part of the river, and this having been effected with so much skill and secrecy as to escape the notice of the Roman soldiers, did them considerable injury; thus Caesar was once more compelled to return without peace or victory. The Romans were, therefore, a third time sent against the Britons; and under

the command of Julius, defeated them near a place called Trinovantum (London), forty-seven years before the birth of Christ, and five thousand two hundred and twelve years from the creation.

Julius was the first exercising supreme power over the Romans who invaded Britain: in honour of him the Romans decreed the fifth month to be called after his name. He was assassinated in the Curia, in the ides of March, and Octavius Augustus succeeded to the empire of the world. He was the only emperor who received tribute from the Britons, according to the following verse of Virgil: "Purpurea intexti tollunt aulaea Britanni."

21. The second after him, who came into Britain, was the emperor Claudius, who reigned forty-seven years after the birth of Christ. He carried with him war and devastation; and, though not without loss of men, he at length conquered Britain. He next sailed to the Orkneys, which he likewise conquered, and afterwards rendered tributary. No tribute was in his time received from the Britons; but it was paid to British emperors. He reigned thirteen years and eight months. His monument is to be seen at Moguntia (among the Lombards), where he died in his way to Rome.

22. After the birth of Christ, one hundred and sixty-seven years, king Lucius, with all the chiefs of the British people, received baptism, in consequence of a legation sent by the Roman emperors and pope Evaristus.*

* V.R. Eucharistus. A marginal note in the Arundel MS. adds, "He is wrong, because the first year of Evaristus was A.D. 79, whereas the first year of Eleutherius, whom he

ought to have named, was A.D. 161." Usher says, that in one MS. of Nennius he found the name of Eleutherius.

23. Severus was the third emperor who passed the sea to Britain, where, to protect the provinces recovered from barbaric incursions, he ordered a wall and a rampart to be made between the Britons, the Scots, and the Picts, extending across the island from sea to sea, in length one hundred and thirty-three miles: and it is called in the British language Gwal.* Moreover, he ordered it to be made between the Britons, and the Picts and Scots; for the Scots from the west, and the Picts from the north, unanimously made war against the Britons; but were at peace among themselves. Not long after Severus dies in Britain.

*Or, the Wall. One MS. here adds, "The above-mentioned Severus constructed it of rude workmanship in length 132 miles; i.e. from Penguaul, which village is called in Scottish Cenail, in English Peneltun, to the mouth of the river Cluth and Cairpentaloch, where this wall terminates; but it was of no avail. The emperor Carausius afterwards rebuilt it, and fortified it with seven castles between the two mouths: he built also a round house of polished stones on the banks of the river Carun (Carron): he likewise erected a triumphal arch, on which he inscribed his own name
in memory of his victory."

24. The fourth was the emperor and tyrant, Carausius, who, incensed at the murder of Severus, passed into Britain, and attended by the leaders of the Roman people, severely

avenged upon the chiefs and rulers of the Britons, the cause of Severus.*

* This passage is corrupt, the meaning is briefly given in the translation.

25. The fifth was Constantius the father of Constantine the Great. He died in Britain; his sepulchre, as it appears by the inscription on his tomb, is still seen near the city named Cair segont (near Carnarvon). Upon the pavement of the above-mentioned city he sowed three seeds of gold, silver and brass, that no poor person might ever be found in it. It is also called Minmanton.*

* V.R. Mirmantum, Mirmantun, Minmanto, Minimantone. The Segontium of Antoninus, situated on a small river named Seiont, near Carnarvon.

26. Maximianus(1) was the sixth emperor that ruled in Britain. It was in his time that consuls(2) began, and that the appellation of Caesar was discontinued: at this period also, St. Martin became celebrated for his virtues and miracles, and held a conversation with him.

(1) This is an inaccuracy of Nennius; Maximus and Maximianus
were one and the same person; or rather no such person as Maximianus ever reigned in Britain. (2) Geoffrey of Monmouth
gives the title of consul to several British generals who lived after this time. It is not unlikely that the town, name, and dignity, still lingered in the provinces after the Romans were gone, particularly as the cities of Britain maintained for a time a species of independence.

27. The seventh emperor was Maximus. He withdrew from Britain with all his military force, slew Gratian, the king of the Romans, and obtained the sovereignty of all Europe. Unwilling to send back his warlike companions to their wives, children, and possessions in Britain, he conferred upon them numerous districts from the lake on the summit of Mons Jovis, to the city called Cant Guic, and to the western Tumulus, that is, to Cruc Occident.* These are the Armoric Britons, and they remain there to the present day. In consequence of their absence, Britain being overcome by foreign nations, the lawful heirs were cast out, till God interposed with his assistance. We are informed by the tradition of our ancestors that seven emperors went into Britain, though the Romans affirm there were nine.

* This district, in modern language, extended from the great St. Bernard in Piedmont to Cantavic in Picardy, and from Picardy to the western coast of France.

28. Thus, aggreeably to the account given by the Britons, the Romans governed them four hundred and nine years.

After this, the Britons despised the authority of the Romans, equally refusing to pay them tribute, or to receive their kings; nor durst the Romans any longer attempt the government of a country, the natives of which massacred their deputies.

29. We must now return to the tyrant Maximus. Gratian, with his brother Valentinian, reigned seven years. Ambrose, bishop of Milan, was then eminent for his skill in the dogmata of the Catholics. Valentinianus and Theodosius reigned eight years. At that time a synod was held at

Constantinople, attended by three hundred and fifty of the fathers, and in which all heresies were condemned. Jerome, the presbyter of Bethlehem, was then universally celebrated. Whilst Gratian exercised supreme dominion over the world, Maximus, in a sedition of the soldiers, was saluted emperor in Britain, and soon after crossed the sea to Gaul. At Paris, by the treachery of Mellobaudes, his master of the horse, Gratian was defeated and fleeing to Lyons, was taken and put to death; Maximus afterwards associated his son victor in the government.

Martin, distinguished for his great virtues, was at this period bishop of Tours. After a considerable space of time, Maximus was divested of royal power by the consuls Valentinianus and Theodosius, and sentenced to be beheaded at the third mile-stone from Aquileia: in the same year also his son Victor was killed in Gaul by Arbogastes, five thousand six hundred and ninety years from the creation of the world.

30. Thrice were the Roman deputies put to death by the Britons, and yet these, when harassed by the incursions of the barbarous nations, viz. Of the Scots and Picts, earnestly solicited the aid of the Romans. To give effect to their entreaties, ambassadors were sent, who made their entrance with impressions of deep sorrow, having their heads covered with dust, and carrying rich presents, to expiate the murder of the deputies. They were favourably received by the consuls, and swore submission to the Roman yoke, with whatever severity it might be imposed.

The Romans, therefore, came with a powerful army to the assistance of the Britons; and having appointed over them a ruler, and settled the government, returned to Rome: and this took place alternately during the space of three hundred and forty-eight years. The Britons, however, from the oppression of the empire, again massacred The Roman deputies, and again petitioned for succour. Once more the Romans undertook the government of the Britons, and assisted them in repelling their neighbours; and, after having exhausted the country of its gold, silver, brass, honey, and costly vestments, and having besides received rich gifts, they returned in great triumph to Rome.

31. After the above-said war between the Britons and Romans, the assassination of their rulers, and the victory of Maximus, who slew Gratian, and the termination of the Roman power in Britain, they were in alarm forty years.

Vortigern then reigned in Britain. In his time, the natives had cause of dread, not only from the inroads of the Scots and Picts, but also from the Romans, and their apprehensions of Ambrosius.*

* These words relate evidently to some cause of dispute between the Romans, Ambrosius, and Vortigern. Vortigern is
said to have been sovereign of the Dimetae, and Ambrosius son to the king of the Damnonii. The latter was half a Roman by descent, and naturally supported the Roman interest: the former was entirely a Briton, and as naturally seconded by the original Britons.

In the meantime, three vessels, exiled from Germany, arrived in Britain. They were commanded by Horsa and Hengist, brothers, and sons of Wihtgils. Wihtgils was the son of Witta; Witta of Wecta; Wecta of Woden; Woden of Frithowald; Frithowald of Frithuwulf; Frithuwulf of Finn; Finn of Godwulf; Godwulf of Geat, who, as they say, was the son of a god, not(1) of the omnipotent God and our Lord Jesus Christ (who before the beginning of the world, was with the Father and the Holy Spirit, co-eternal and of the same substance, and who, in compassion to human nature, disdained not to assume the form of a servant), but the offspring of one of their idols, and whom, blinded by some demon, they worshipped according to the custom of the heathen. Vortigern received them as friends, and delivered up to them the island which is in their language called Thanet, and, by the Britons, Ruym.(2) Gratianus Aequantius at that time reigned in Rome. The Saxons were received by Vortigern, four hundred and forty-seven years after the passion of Christ, and,(3) according to the tradition of our ancestors, from the period of their first arrival in Britain, to the first year of the reign of king Edmund, five hundred and forty-two years; and to that in which we now write, which is the fifth of his reign, five hundred and forty-seven years.

(1) V.R. not the God of gods, the Amen, the Lord of Hosts, but one of their idols which they worshipped.

(2) Sometimes called Ruoichin, Ruith-in, or "river island," separated from the rest of Kent and the mainland of Britain by the estuary of the Wantsum, which, though now a small

brook, was formerly navigable for large vessels, and in Bede's time was three stadia broad, and fordable only at two places.

(3) The rest of this sentence is omitted in some of the MSS.

32. At that time St. Germanus, distinguished for his numerous virtues, came to preach in Britain: by his ministry many were saved; but many likewise died unconverted. Of the various miracles which God enabled him to perform, I shall here mention only a few: I shall first advert to that concerning an iniquitous and tyrannical king, named Benlli.* The holy man, informed of his wicked conduct, hastened to visit him, for the purpose of remonstrating him. When the man of God, with his attendants, arrived at the gate of the city, they were respectfully received by the keeper of it, who came out and saluted them. Him they commissioned to communicate their intention to the king, who returned a harsh answer, declaring, with an oath, that although they remained there a year, they should not enter the city. While waiting for an answer, the evening came on, and they knew not where to go. At length, came one of the king's servants, who bowing himself before the man of God, announced the words of the tyrant, inviting them, at the same time, to his own house, to which they went, and were kindly received. It happened, however, that he had no cattle, except one cow and a calf, the latter of which, urged by generous hospitality to his guests, he killed, dressed and set before them. But holy St. Germanus ordered his companions not to break a bone of

the calf; and, the next morning, it was found alive uninjured, and standing by its mother.

* King of Powys. V.R. Benli in the district of Ial (in Derbyshire); in the district of Dalrieta; Belinus; Beluni; and Benty.

33. Early the same day, they again went to the gate of the city, to solicit audience of the wicked king; and, whilst engaged in fervent prayer they were waiting for admission, a man, covered with sweat, came out, and prostrated himself before them. Then St. Germanus, addressing him, said "Dost thou believe in the Holy Trinity?" To which the man having replied, "I do believe," he baptized, and kissed him, saying, "Go in peace; within this hour thou shalt die: the angels of God are waiting for thee in the air; with them thou shalt ascent to that God in whom thou has believed." He, overjoyed, entered the city, and being met by the prefect, was seized, bound, and conducted before the tyrant, who having passed sentence upon him, he was immediately put to death; for it was a law of this wicked king, that whoever was not at his labour before sun-rising should be beheaded in the citadel. In the meantime, St. Germanus, with his attendants, waited the whole day before the gate, without obtaining admission to the tyrant.

34. The man above-mentioned, however, remained with them. "Take care," said St. Germanus to him, "that none of your friends remain this night within these walls." Upon this he hastily entered the city, brought out his nine sons, and with them retired to the house where he had exercised such generous hospitality. Here St. Germanus ordered them to

continue, fasting; and when the gates were shut, "Watch," said he, "and whatever shall happen in the citadel, turn not thither your eyes; but pray without ceasing, and invoke the protection of the true God." And, behold, early in the night, fire fell from heaven, and burned the city, together with all those who were with the tyrant, so that not one escaped; and that citadel has never been rebuilt even to this day.

35. The following day, the hospitable man who had been converted by the preaching of St. Germanus, was baptized, with his sons, and all the inhabitants of that part of the country; and St. Germanus blessed him, saying, "a king shall not be wanting of thy seed for ever." The name of this person is Catel Drunlue:* "from henceforward thou shalt be a king all the days of thy life." Thus was fulfilled the prophecy of the Psalmist: "He raiseth up the poor out of the dust, and lifteth up the needy out of the dunghill." And agreeably to the prediction of St. Germanus, from a servant he became a king: all his sons were kings, and from their offspring the whole country of Powys has been governed to this day.

* Or Cadell Deyrnllug, prince of the Vale Royal and the upper part of Powys.

36. After the Saxons had continued some time in the island of Thanet, Vortigern promised to supply them with clothing and provision, on condition they would engage to fight against the enemies of his country. But the barbarians having greatly increased in number, the Britons became incapable of fulfilling their engagement; and when the Saxons, according to the promise they had received, claimed a supply of provisions and clothing, the Britons replied,

"Your number is increased; your assistance is now unneccessary; you may, therefore, return home, for we can no longer support you;" and hereupon they began to devise means of breaking the peace between them.

37. But Hengist, in whom united craft and penetration, perceiving he had to act with an ignorant king, and a fluctuating people, incapable of opposing much resistance, replied to Vortigern, "We are, indeed, few in number; but, if you will give us leave, we will send to our country for an additional number of forces, with whom we will fight for you and your subjects." Vortigern assenting to this proposal, messengers were despatched to Scythia, where selecting a number of warlike troops, they returned with sixteen vessels, bringing with them the beautiful daughter of Hengist. And now the Saxon chief prepared an entertainment, to which he invited the king, his officers, and Ceretic, his interpreter, having previously enjoined his daughter to serve them so profusely with wine and ale, that they might soon become intoxicated. This plan succeeded; and Vortigern, at the instigation of the devil, and enamoured with the beauty of the damsel, demanded her, through the medium of his interpreter, of the father, promising to give for her whatever he should ask. Then Hengist, who had already consulted with the elders who attended him of the Oghgul(1) race, demanded for his daughter the province, called in English, Centland, in British, Ceint, (Kent.) This cession was made without the knowledge of the king, Guoyrancgonus,(2) who then reigned in Kent, and who experienced no inconsiderable share of grief, from seeing his

kingdom thus clandestinely, fraudulently, and imprudently resigned to foreigners. Thus the maid was delivered up to the king, who slept with her, and loved her exceedingly.

(1) V.R. Who had come with him from the island of Oghgul, Oehgul (or Tingle), Angul. According to Gunn, a small island in the duchy of Sleswick in Denmark, now called Angel, of which Flensburg is the metropolis. Hence the origin of the Angles.

(2) V.R. Gnoiram cono, Goiranegono, Guiracgono. Malmesbury,
Gorongi; Camden, Guorong, supposed to mean governor, or viceroy.

38. Hengist, after this, said to Vortigern, "I will be to you both a father and an adviser; despise not my counsels, and you shall have no reason to fear being conquered by any man or any nation whatever; for the people of my country are strong, warlike, and robust: if you approve, I will send for my son and his brother, both valiant men, who at my invitation will fight against the Scots, and you can give them the countries in the north, near the wall called Gual."(1) The incautious sovereign having assented to this, Octa and Ebusa arrived with forty ships. In these they sailed round the country of the Picts, laid waste the Orkneys, and took possession of many regions, even to the Pictish confines.(2)

(1) Antoninus's wall.

(2) Some MSS. add, "beyond the Frenesic, Fresicum (or Fresic) sea," i.e. which is between us and the Scotch. The

sea between Scotland and Ireland. Camden translates it "beyond the Frith;" Langhorne says, "Solway Frith."

But Hengist continued, by degrees, sending for ships from his own country, so that some islands whence they came were left without inhabitants; and whilst his people were increasing in power and number, they came to the above-named province of Kent.

39. In the meantime, Vortigern, as if desirous of adding to the evils he had already occasioned, married his own daughter, by whom he had a son. When this was made known to St. Germanus, he came, with all the British clergy, to reprove him: and whilst a numerous assembly of the ecclesiastics and laity were in consultation, the weak king ordered his daughter to appear before them, and in the presence of all to present her son to St. Germanus, and declare that he was the father of the child. The immodest* woman obeyed; and St. Germanus, taking the child, said, "I will be a father to you, my son; nor will I dismiss you till a razor, scissors, and comb, are given to me, and it is allowed you to give them to your carnal father." The child obeyed St. Germanus, and going to his father Vortigern, said to him, "Thou art my father; shave and cut the hair of my head." The king blushed, and was silent; and, without replying to the child, arose in great anger, and fled from the presence of St. Germanus, execrated and condemned by the whole synod.

(1) V.R. "Immodest" is omitted in some MSS.

40. But soon after, calling together his twelve wise men, to consult what was to be done, they said to him, "Retire to the remote boundaries of your kingdom; there build and fortify

a city(1) to defend yourself, for the people you have received are treacherous; they are seeking to subdue you by stratagem, and, even during your life, to seize upon all the countries subject to your power, how much more will they attempt, after your death!" The king, pleased with this advice, departed with his wise men, and travelled through many parts of his territories, in search of a place convenient for the purpose of building a citadel. Having, to no purpose, travelled far and wide, they came at length to a province called Guenet;(2) and having surveyed the mountains of Heremus,(3) they discovered, on the summit of one of them, a situation, adapted to the construction of a citadel. Upon this, the wise men said to the king, "Build here a city: for, in this place, it will ever be secure against the barbarians." Then the king sent for artificers, carpenters, stone-masons, and collected all the materials requisite to building; but the whole of these disappeared in one night, so that nothing remained of what had been provided for the constructing of the citadel. Materials were, therefore, from all parts, procured a second and third time, and again vanished as before, leaving and rendering every effort ineffectual. Vortigern inquired of his wise men the cause of this opposition to his undertaking, and of so much useless expense of labour? They replied, "You must find a child born without a father, put him to death, and sprinkle with his blood the ground on which the citadel is to be built, or you will never accomplish your purpose."

(1) V.R. You shall find a fortified city in which you may defend yourself.

(2) V.R. Guined, Guoienet, Guenez, North Wales.

(3) V.R. Heremi, Heriri, or Eryri, signifying eagle rocks, the mountains of Snowdon, in Carnarvonshire. The spot alluded to is supposed to be Dinas Emrys, or the fortress of Ambrosius.

41. In consequence of this reply, the king sent messengers throughout Britain, in search of a child born without a father. After having inquired in all the provinces, they came to the field of Aelecti,(1) in the district of Glevesing,(2) where a party of boys were playing at ball. And two of them quarrelling, one said to the other, "O boy without a father, no good will ever happen to you." Upon this, the messengers diligently inquired of the mother and the other boys, whether he had had a father? Which his mother denied, saying, "In what manner he was conceived I know not, for I have never had intercourse with any man;" and then she solemnly affirmed that he had no mortal father. The boy was, therefore, led away, and conducted before Vortigern the king.

(1) V.R. Elleti, Electi, Gleti. Supposed to be Bassalig in Monmouthshire.

(2) The district between the Usk and Rumney, in Monmouthshire.

42. A meeting took place the next day for the purpose of putting him to death. Then the boy said to the king, "Why have your servants brought me hither?" "That you may be

put to death," replied the king, "and that the ground on which my citadel is to stand, may be sprinkled with your blood, without which I shall be unable to build it." "Who," said the boy, "instructed you to do this?" "My wise men," answered the king. "Order them hither," returned the boy; this being complied with, he thus questioned them: "By what means was it revealed to you that this citadel could not be built, unless the spot were previously sprinkled with my blood? Speak without disguise, and declare who discovered me to you;" then turning to the king, "I will soon," said he, "unfold to you every thing; but I desire to question your wise men, and wish them to disclose to you what is hidden under this pavement:" they acknowledging their ignorance, "there is," said he, "a pool; come and dig:" they did so, and found the pool. "Now," continued he, "tell me what is in it;" but they were ashamed, and made no reply. "I," said the boy, "can discover it to you: there are two vases in the pool;" they examined and found it so: continuing his questions, "What is in the vases?" they were silent: "there is a tent in them," said the boy; "separate them, and you shall find it so;" this being done by the king's command, there was found in them a folded tent. The boy, going on with his questions, asked the wise men what was in it? But they not knowing what to reply, "There are," said he, "two serpents, one white and the other red; unfold the tent;" they obeyed, and two sleeping serpents were discovered; "consider attentively," said the boy, "what they are doing." The serpents began to struggle with each other; and the white one, raising himself up, threw down the other into the middle of the tent, and sometimes drove him to the edge of it; and this was repeated thrice. At length the red one, apparently the weaker of the two, recovering his strength, expelled the white one from the tent; and the latter being pursued through the pool by the red one, disappeared. Then the boy, asking the wise men what was signified by this wonderful omen, and they expressing their ignorance, he said to the king, "I will now unfold to you the meaning of this mystery. The pool is the emblem of this world, and the tent that of your kingdom: the two serpents are two dragons; the red serpent is your dragon, but the white serpent is the dragon of the people who occupy several provinces and districts of Britain, even almost from sea to sea: at length, however, our people shall rise and drive away the Saxon race from beyond the sea, whence they originally came; but do you depart from this place, where you are not permitted to erect a citadel; I, to whom fate has allotted this mansion, shall remain here; whilst to you it is incumbent to seek other provinces, where you may build a fortress." "What is your name?" asked the king; "I am called Ambrose (in British Embresguletic)," returned the boy; and in answer to the king's question, "What is your origin?" he replied, "A Roman consul was my father."

Then the king assigned him that city, with all the western Provinces of Britain; and departing with his wise men to the sinistral district, he arrived in the region named Gueneri, where he built a city which, according to his name, was called Cair Guorthegirn.*

* An ancient scholiast adds, "He then built Guasmoric, near Lugubalia (Carlisle), a city which in English is called Palmecaster." Some difference of opinion exists among antiquaries respecting the site of vortigern's castle or city. Usher places it at Gwent, Monmouthshire, which name, he ways, was taken from Caer-Went, near Chepstow. This appears to agree with Geoffrey's account, {illegible} See Usher's Britan. Eccles. cap. v. p.23. According to others, supposed to be the city from the ruins of which arose the castle of Gurthrenion, in Radnorshire, Camden's Britannia, p.479. Whitaker, however, says that Cair Guorthegirn was the Maridunum of the Romans, and the present Caermarthen.
(Hist. Of Manchester, book ii. c. 1.) See also Nennius, sec.47.

43. At length Vortimer, the son of Vortigern, valiantly fought against Hengist, Horsa, and his people; drove them to the isle of Thanet, and thrice enclosed them within it, and beset them on the Western side.

The Saxons now despatched deputies to Germany to solicit large reinforcements, and an additional number of ships: having obtained these, they fought against the kings and princes of Britain, and sometimes extended their boundaries by victory, and sometimes were conquered and driven back.

44. Four times did Vortimer valorously encounter the enemy;(1) the first has been mentioned, the second was upon the river Darent, the third at the Ford, in their language called Epsford, though in ours Set thirgabail,(2) there Horsa

fell, and Catigern, the son of Vortigern; the fourth battle he fought was near the stone(3) on the shore of the Gallic sea, where the Saxons being defeated, fled to their ships.

(1) Some MSS. here add, "This Vortimer, the son of Vortigern, in a synod held at Guartherniaun, after the wicked king, on account of the incest committed with his daughter, fled from the face of Germanus and the British clergy, would not consent to his father's wickedness; but returning to St. Germanus, and falling down at his feet, he sued for pardon; and in atonement for the calumny brought upon Germanus by his father and sister, gave him the land, in which the forementioned bishop had endured such abuse, to
be his for ever. Whence, in memory of St. Germanus, it received the name Guarenniaun (Guartherniaun, Gurthrenion,
Gwarth Ennian) which signifies, a calumny justly retorted, since, when he thought to reproach the bishop, he covered himself with reproach."

(2) According to Langhorne, Epsford was afterwards called, in the British tongue, Saessenaeg habail, or 'the slaughter of the Saxons.'

(3) V.R. "The Stone of Titulus", thought to be Stone in Kent, or Larger-stone in Suffolk.

After a short interval Vortimer died; before his decease, anxious for the future prosperity of his country, he charged his friends to inter his body at the entrance of the Saxon port, viz. upon the rock where the Saxons first landed; "for though," said he, "they may inhabit other parts of Britain, yet if you follow my commands, they will never remain in this island." They imprudently disobeyed this last injunction, and neglected to bury him where he had appointed.*

* Rapin says he was buried at Lincoln; Geoffrey, at London.

45. After this the barbarians became firmly incorporated, and were assisted by foreign pagans; for Vortigern was their friend, on account of the daughter* of Hengist, whom he so much loved, that no one durst fight against him-in the meantime they soothed the imprudent king, and whilst practising every appearance of fondness, were plotting with his enemies. And let him that reads understand, that the Saxons were victorious, and ruled Britain, not from their superior prowess, but on account of the great sins of the Britons: God so permitting it.

For what wise man will resist the wholesome counsel of God? The Almighty is the King of kings, and the Lord of lords, ruling and judging every one, according to his own pleasure.

After the death of Vortimer, Hengist being strengthened by new accessions, collected his ships, and calling his leaders together, consulted by what stratagem they might overcome Vortigern and his army; with insidious intention they sent messengers to the king, with offers of peace and perpetual friendship; unsuspicious of treachery, the monarch, after advising with his elders, accepted the proposals.

* V.R. Of his wife, and no one was able manfully to drive them off because they had occupied Britain not from their own valour, but by God's permission.

46. Hengist, under pretence of ratifying the treaty, prepared an entertainment, to which he invited the king, the nobles, and military officers, in number about three hundred; speciously concealing his wicked intention, he ordered three hundred Saxons to conceal each a knife under his feet, and to mix with the Britons; "and when," said he, "they are sufficiently inebriated, &c. cry out, 'Nimed eure Saxes,' then let each draw his knife, and kill his man; but spare the king, on account of his marriage with my daughter, for it is better that he should be ransomed than killed."*

* The VV. RR. Of this section are too numerous to be inserted.

The king with his company, appeared at the feast; and mixing with the Saxons, who, whilst they spoke peace with their tongues, cherished treachery in their hearts, each man was placed next to his enemy.

After they had eaten and drunk, and were much intoxicated, Hengist suddenly vociferated, "Nimed eure Saxes!" and instantly his adherents drew their knives, and rushing upon the Britons, each slew him that sat next to him, and there was slain three hundred of the nobles of Vortigern. The king being a captive, purchased his redemption, by delivering up the three provinces of East, South, and Middle Sex, besides other districts at the option of his betrayers.

47. St. Germanus admonished Vortigern to turn to the true God, and abstain from all unlawful intercourse with his daughter; but the unhappy wretch fled for refuge to the province Guorthegirnaim,* so called from his own name, where he concealed himself with his wives: but St. Germanus

followed him with all the British clergy, and upon a rock prayed for his sins during forty days and forty nights.

* A district of Radnorshire, forming the present hundred of Rhaiadr.

The Blessed man was unanimously chosen commander against the Saxons. And then, not by the clang of trumpets, but by praying, singing hallelujah, and by the cries of the army to God, the enemies were routed, and driven even to the sea.*

*V.R. This paragraph is omitted in the MSS.

Again Vortigern ignominiously flew from St. Germanus to the kingdom of the Dimetae, where, on the river Towy,* he built a castle, which he named Cair Guothergirn. The saint, as usual, followed him there, and with his clergy fasted and prayed to the Lord three days, and as many nights. On the third night, at the third hour, fire fell suddenly from heaven, and totally burned the castle. Vortigern, the daughter of Hengist, his other wives, and all the inhabitants, both men and women, miserably perished: such was the end of this unhappy king, as we find written in the life of St. Germanus.

*The Tobias of Ptolemy

47. Others assure us, that being hated by all the people of Britain, for having received the Saxons, and being publicly charged by St. Germanus and the clergy in the sight of God, he betook himself to flight; and, that deserted and a wanderer, he sought a place of refuge, till broken hearted, he made an ignominious end.

Some accounts state, that the earth opened and swallowed him up, on the night his castle was burned; as no remains were discovered the following morning, either of him, or of those who were burned with him.

He had three sons: the eldest was Vortimer, who, as we have seen, fought four times against the Saxons, and put them to flight; the second Categirn, who was slain in the same battle with Horsa; the third was Pascent, who reigned in the two provinces Builth and Guorthegirnaim,(1) after the death of his father. These were granted him by Ambrosius, who was the great king among the kings of Britain. The fourth was Faustus, born of an incestuous marriage with his daughter, who was brought up and educated by St. Germanus. He built a large monastery on the banks of the river Renis, called after his name, and which remains to the present period.(2)

(1) In the northern part of the present counties of Radnor and Brecknock.

(2) V.R. The MSS. add, 'and he had one daughter, who was the
mother of St. Faustus.'

49. This is the genealogy of Vortigern, which goes back to Fernvail,(1) who reigned in the kingdom of Guorthegirnaim,(2) and was the son of Teudor; Teudor was the son of Pascent; Pascent of Guoidcant; Guoidcant of Moriud; Moriud of Eltat; Eltat of Eldoc; Eldoc of Paul; Paul of Meuprit; Meuprit of Braciat; Braciat of Pascent; Pascent of Guorthegirn, Guorthegirn of Guortheneu; Guortheneu of

Guitaul; Guitaul of Guitolion; Guitolion of Gloui. Bonus, Paul, Mauron, Guotelin, were four brothers, who built Gloiuda, a great city upon the banks of the river Severn, and in Birtish is called Cair Gloui, in Saxon, Gloucester. Enough has been said of Vortigern.

(1) Fernvail, or Farinmail, appears to have been king of Gwent or Monmouth.

(2) V.R. 'Two provinces, Builth and Guorthegirnaim.'

50. St. Germanus, after his death, returned into his own country. *At that time, the Saxons greatly increased in Britain, both in strength and numbers. And Octa, after the death of his father Hengist, came from the sinistral part of the island to the kingdom of Kent, and from him have proceeded all the kings of that province, to the present period.

* V.R. All this to the word 'Amen,' in other MSS. is placed after the legend of St. Patrick.

Then it was, that the magnanimous Arthur, with all the kings and military force of Britain, fought against the Saxons. And though there were many more noble than himself, yet he was twelve times chosen their commander, and was as often conqueror. The first battle in which he was engaged, was at the mouth of the river Gleni.(1) The second, third, fourth, and fifth, were on another river, by the Britons called Duglas,(2) in the region Linuis. The sixth, on the river Bassas.(3) The seventh in the wood Celidon, which the Britons call Cat Coit Celidon.(4) The eighth was near Gurnion castle,(5) where Arthur bore the image of the Holy Virgin,(6) mother of God, upon his shoulders, and through the power of our Lord Jesus Christ, and the holy Mary, put the Saxons to flight, and pursued them the whole day with great slaughter.(7) The ninth was at the City of Legion,(8) which is called Cair Lion. The tenth was on the banks of the river Trat Treuroit.(9) The eleventh was on the mountain Breguoin, which we call Cat Bregion.(10) The twelfth was a most severe contest, when Arthur penetrated to the hill of Badon.(11) In this engagement, nine hundred and forty fell by his hand alone, no one but the Lord affording him assistance. In all these engagements the Britons were successful. For no strength can avail against the will of the Almighty.

(1) Supposed by some to be the Glem, in Lincolnshire; but most probably the Glen, in the northern part of Northumberland.

(2) Or Dubglas. The little river Dunglas, which formed the southern boundary of Lothian. Whitaker says, the river Duglas, in Lancashire, near Wigan.

(3) Not a river, but an isolated rock in the Frith of Forth, near the town of North Berwick, called "The Bass." Some think it is the river Lusas, in Hampshire.

(4) The Caledonian forest; or the forest of Englewood, extending from Penrith to Carlisle.

(5) Variously supposed to be in Cornwall, or Binchester in

Durham, but most probably the Roman station of Garionenum,
near Yarmouth, in Norfolk.

(6) V.R. The image of the cross of Christ, and of the perpetual virgin St. Mary.

(7) V.R. For Arthur proceeded to Jerusalem, and there made a
cross to the size of the Saviour's cross, and there it was consecrated, and for three successive days he fasted, watched, and prayed, before the Lord's cross, that the Lord would give him the victory, by this sign, over the heathen; which also took place, and he took with him the image of St. Mary, the fragments of which are still preserved in great veneration at Wedale, in English Wodale, in Latin Vallis-doloris. Wodale is a village in the province of Lodonesia, but now of the jurisdiction of the bishop of St. Andrew's, of Scotland, six miles on the west of that heretofore noble and eminent monastery of Meilros.

(8) Exeter.

(9) Or Ribroit, the Brue, in Somersetshire; or the Ribble, in Lancashire.

(10) Or Agned Cathregonion, Cadbury, in Somersetshire; or Edinburgh

(11) Bath.

The more the Saxons were vanquished, the more they sought for new supplies of Saxons from Germany; so that kings, commanders, and military bands were invited over from almost every province. And this practice they continued till the reign of Ida, who was the son of Eoppa, he, of the Saxon race, was the first king in Bernicia, and in Cair Ebrauc (York).

When Gratian Aequantius was consul at rome, because then the whole world was governed by the Roman consuls, the Saxons were received by Vortigern in the year of our Lord four hundred and forty-seven, and to the year in which we now write, five hundred and forty-seven. And whosoever shall read herein may receive instruction, the Lord Jesus Christ affording assistance, who, co-eternal with the Father and the Holy Ghost, lives and reigns for ever and ever. Amen.

In those days Saint Patrick was captive among the Scots. His master's name was Milcho, to whom he was a swineherd for seven years. When he had attained the age of seventeen he gave him his liberty. By the divine impulse, he applied himself to reading of the Scriptures, and afterwards went to Rome; where, replenished with the Holy Spirit, he continued a great while, studying the sacred mysteries of those writings. During his continuance there, Palladius, the first bishop, was sent by pope Celestine to convert the Scots (the Irish). But tempests and signs from God prevented his landing, for no one can arrive in any country, except it be allowed from above; altering therefore his course from Ireland, he came to Britain and died in the land of the Picts.*

* At Fordun, in the district of Mearns, in Scotland-Usher.

51. The death of Palladius being known, the Roman patricians, Theodosius and Valentinian, then reigning, pope Celestine sent Patrick to convert the Scots to the faith of the Holy Trinity; Victor, the angel of God, accompanying, admonishing, and assisting him, and also the bishop Germanus.

Germanus then sent the ancient Segerus with him as a venerable and praiseworthy bishop, to king Amatheus,(1) who lived near, and who had prescience of what was to happen; he was consecrated bishop in the reign of that king by the holy pontiff,(2) assuming the name of Patrick, having hitherto been known by that of Maun; Auxilius, Isserninus, and other brothers were ordained with him to inferior degrees.

(1) V.R. Germanus "sent the elder Segerus with him to a wonderful man, the holy bishop Amathearex." Another MS. "Sent the elder Segerus, a bishop, with him to Amatheorex."

(2) V.R. "Received the episcopal degree from the holy bishop Amatheorex." Another MS. "Received the episcopal degree from Matheorex and the holy bishop."

52. Having distributed benedictions, and perfected all in the name of the Holy Trinity, he embarked on the sea which is between the Gauls and the Britons; and after a quick passage arrived in Britain, where he preached for some time. Every necessary preparation being made, and the angel

giving him warning, he came to the Irish Sea. And having filled the ship with foreign gifts and spiritual treasures, by the permission of God he arrived in Ireland, where he baptized and preached.

53. From the beginning of the world, to the fifth year of king Logiore, when the Irish were baptized, and faith in the unity of the individual Trinity was published to them, are five thousand three hundred and thirty years.

54. Saint Patrick taught the gospel in foreign nations for the space of forty years. Endued with apostolical powers, he gave sight to the blind, cleansed the lepers, gave hearing to the deaf, cast out devils, raised nine from the dead, redeemed many captives of both sexes at his own charge, and set them free in the name of the Holy Trinity. He taught the servants of God, and he wrote three hundred and sixty-five canonical and other books relating to the catholic faith. He founded as many churches, and consecrated the same number of bishops, strengthening them with the Holy Ghost. He ordained three thousand presbyters; and converted and baptized twelve thousand persons in the province of Connaught. And, in one day baptized seven kings, who were the seven sons of Amalgaid.(1) He continued fasting forty days and nights, on the summit of the mountain Eli, that is Cruachan-Aichle;(2) and preferred three petitions to God for the Irish, that had embraced the faith. The Scots say, the first was, that he would receive every repenting sinner, even at the latest extremity of life; the second, that they should never be exterminated by barbarians; and the third, that as Ireland(3) will be overflowed with water, seven years before

the coming of our Lord to judge the quick and the dead, the crimes of the people might be washed away through his intercession, and their souls purified at the last day. He gave the people his benediction from the upper part of the mountain, and going up higher, that he might pray for them; and that if it pleased God, he might see the effects of his labours, there appeared to him an innumerable flock of birds of many coulours, signifying the number of holy persons of both sexes of the Irish nation, who should come to him as their apostle at the day of judgment, to be presented before the tribunal of Christ. After a life spent in the active exertion of good to mankind, St. Patrick, in a healthy old age, passed from this world to the Lord, and changing this life for a better, with the saints and elect of God he rejoices for evermore.

(1) King of Connaught.

(2) A mountain in the west of Connaught, county of Mayo, now
called Croagh-Patrick.

(3) V.R. that no Irishman may be alive on the day of
judgment, because they will be destroyed seven years before
in honour of St. Patrick.

55. Saint Patrick resembled Moses in four particulars. The angel spoke to him in the burning bush. He fasted forty days and forty nights upon the mountain. He attained the period of one hundred and twenty years. No one knows his

sepulchre, nor where he was buried; sixteen(1) years he was in captivity. In his twenty-fifth year, he was consecrated bishop by Saint Matheus,(2) and he was eighty-five years the apostle of the Irish. It might be profitable to treat more at large of the life of this saint, but it is now time to conclude this epitome of his labours.(3)

(1) V.R. Fifteen.

(2) V.R. By the holy bishop Amatheus.

(3) Here ends the Vatican MS. collated by Mr. Gunn.
(Here endeth the life of the holy bishop, Saint Patrick.) (After this, the MSS. give as 56, the legend of king Arthur, which in this edition occurs in 50.)

THE GENEALOGY OF THE KINGS OF BERNICIA.*

* These titles are not part of the original work, but added in the MSS. by a later hand.

57. Woden begat Beldeg, who begat Beornec, who begat Gethbrond, who begat Aluson, who begat Ingwi, who begat Edibrith, who begat Esa, who begat Eoppa, who begat Ida. But Ida had twelve sons, Adda, Belric, Theodric, Ethelric, Theodhere, Osmer, and one queen, Bearnoch, Ealric. Ethelric begat Ethelfrid: the same is Aedlfred Flesaur. For he also had seven sons, Eanfrid, Oswald, Oswin, Oswy, Oswudu, Oslac, Offa. Oswy begat Alfrid, Elfwin, and Egfrid. Egfrid is he who

made war against his cousin Brudei, king of the Picts, and he fell therein with all the strength of his army, and the Picts with their king gained the victory; and the Saxons never again reduced the Picts so as to exact tribute from them. Since the time of this war it is called Gueithlin Garan.

But Oswy had two wives, Riemmelth, the daughter of Royth, son of Rum; and Eanfled, the daughter of Edwin, son of Alla.

THE GENEALOGY OF THE KINGS OF KENT.

58. Hengist begat Octa, who begat Ossa, who begat Eormenric, who begat Ethelbert, who begat Eadbald, who begat Ercombert, who begat Egbert.

THE ORIGIN OF THE KINGS OF EAST-ANGLIA.

59. Woden begat Casser, who begat Titinon, who begat Trigil, who begat Rodmunt, who begat Rippa, who begat Guillem Guercha,* who was the first king of the East Angles. Guercha begat Uffa, who begat Tytillus, who begat Eni, who begat Edric, who begat Aldwulf, who begat Elric.

* Guercha is a distortion of the name of Uffa, or Wuffa, arising in the first instance from the pronunciation of the

British writer; and in the next place from the error of the transcriber—Palgrave.

THE GENEALOGY OF THE MERCIANS.

60. Woden begat Guedolgeat, who begat Gueagon, who begat Guithleg, who begat Guerdmund, who begat Ossa, who begat Ungen, who begat Eamer, who begat Pubba.* This Pubba had twelve sons, of whom two are better known to me than the others, that is Penda and Eawa. Eadlit is the son of Pantha, Penda, son of Pubba, Ealbald, son of Alguing, son of Eawa, son of Penda, son of Pubba. Egfert, son of Offa, son of Thingferth, son of Enwulf, son of Ossulf, son of Eawa, son of Pubba.

* Or Wibba.

THE KINGS OF THE DEIRI.

61. Woden begat Beldeg, Brond begat Siggar, who begat Sibald, who begat Zegulf, who begat Soemil, who first separated(1) Deur from Berneich (Deira from Bernicia.) Soemil begat Sguerthing, who begat Giulglis, who begat Ulfrea, who begat Iffi, who begat Ulli, Edwin, Osfrid and Eanfrid. There were two sons of Edwin, who fell with him in battle at Meicen,(2) and the kingdom was never renewed in

his family, because not one of his race escaped from that war; but all were slain with him by the army of Catguollaunus,(3) king of the Guendota. Oswy begat Egfrid, the same is Ailguin, who begat Oslach, sho begat Alhun, who begat Adlsing, who begat Echun, who begat Oslaph. Ida begat Eadric, who begat Ecgulf, who begat Leodwald, who begat Eata, the same is Glinmaur, who begat Eadbert and Egbert, who was the first bishop of their nation.

(1) V.R. Conquered.

(2) Hatfield, in the West Riding of Yorkshire. See Bede's Eccles. Hist.

(3) Cadwalla, king of the Western Britons.

Ida, the son of Eoppa, possessed countries on the left-hand side of Britain, i.e. of the Humbrian sea, and reigned twelve years, and united* Dynguayth Guarth-Berneich.

* V.R. United the castle, i.e. Dinguerin and Gurdbernech, which two countries were in one country, i.e. Deurabernech; Anglice Diera and Bernicia. Another MS. Built Dinguayrh Guarth Berneich.

62. Then Dutgirn at that time fought bravely against the nation of the Angles. At that time, Talhaiarn Cataguen* was famed for poetry, and Neirin, and Taliesin and Bluchbard, and Cian, who is called Guenith Guaut, were all famous at the same time in British poetry.

* Talhaiarn was a descendant of Coel Godebog, and chaplain to Ambrosius.

The great king, Mailcun,* reigned among the Britons, i.e. in the district of Guenedota, because his great-great-grandfather, Cunedda, with his twelve sons, had come before from the left-hand part, i.e. from the country which is called Manau Gustodin, one hundred and forty-six years before Mailcun reigned, and expelled the Scots with much slaughter from those countries, and they never returned again to inhabit them.

* Better known as Maelgwn.

63. Adda, son of Ida, reigned eight years; Ethelric, son of Adda, reigned four years. Theodoric, son of Ida, reigned seven years. Freothwulf reigned six years. In whose time the kingdom of Kent, by the mission of Gregory, received baptism. Hussa reigned seven years. Against him fought four kings, Urien, and Ryderthen, and Guallauc, and Morcant. Theodoric fought bravely, together with his sons, against that Urien. But at that time sometimes the enemy and sometimes our countrymen were defeated, and he shut them up three days and three nights in the island of Metcaut; and whilst he was on an expedition he was murdered, at the instance of Morcant, out of envy, because he possessed so much superiority over all the kings in military science. Eadfered Flesaurs reigned twelve years in Bernicia, and twelve others in Deira, and gave to his wife Bebba, the town of Dynguaroy, which from her is called Bebbanburg.*

* Bambrough. See Bede, iii. 6, and Sax. Chron. A.D. 547.

Edwin, son of Alla, reigned seventeen years, seized on Elmete, and expelled Cerdic, its king. Eanfled, his daughter, received baptism, on the twelfth day after Pentecost, with all her followers, both men and women. The following Easter Edwin himself received baptism, and twelve thousand of his subjects with him. If any one wishes to know who baptized them, it was Rum Map Urbgen:* he was engaged forty days in baptizing all classes of the Saxons, and by his preaching many believed on Christ.

* See Bede's Eccles. Hist. From the share which Paulinus had in the conversion of the Northumbrian king, it has been inferred that he actually baptized him; but Nennius expressly states, that the holy sacrament was administered by Rhun, the son of Urien. The Welsh name of Paulinus is Pawl Hen, or Polin Eagob.

64. Oswald son of Ethelfrid, reigned nine years; the same is Oswald Llauiguin;(1) he slew Catgublaun (Cadwalla),(2) king of Guenedot,(3) in the battle of Catscaul,(4) with much loss to his own army. Oswy, son of Ethelfrid, reigned twenty-eight years and six months. During his reign, there was a dreadful mortality among his subjects, when Catgualart (Cadwallader) was king among the Britons, succeeding his father, and he himself died amongst the rest.(5) He slew Penda in the field of Gai, and now took place the slaughter of Gai Campi, and the kings of the Britons, who went out with Penda on the expedition as far as the city of Judeu, were slain.

(1) Llauiguin, means the "fair," or the "bounteous hand."

(2) This name has been variously written; Bede spells it Caedualla (Cadwalla); Nennius, Catgublaun; the Saxon Chronicle, Ceadwalla; and the Welsh writers, Cadwallon and

Kalwallawn: and though the identity of the person may be clearly proved, it is necessary to observe these particulars to distinguish him from Cadwaladr, and from another Caedualla or Caedwalla, a king of the West Saxons; all of whom, as they lived within a short time of each other, have been frequently confounded together.—Rees's Welsh Saints.

(3) Gwynedd, North Wales.

(4) Bede says at Denis's brook.

(5) The British chronicles assert that Cadwallader died at Rome, whilst Nennius would lead us to conclude that he perished in the pestilence at home.

65. Then Oswy restored all the wealth, which was with him in the city, to Penda; who distributed it among the kings of the Britons, that is Atbert Judeu. But Catgabail alone, king of Guenedot, rising up in the night, excaped, together with his army, wherefore he was called Catgabail Catguommed. Egfrid, son of Oswy, reigned nine years. In his time the holy bishop Cuthbert died in the island of Medcaut.* It was he who made war against the Picts, and was by them slain.
* The isle of Farne.

Penda, son of Pybba, reigned ten years; he first separated the kingdom of Mercia from that of the North-men, and slew by treachery Anna, king of the East Anglians, and St. Oswald, king of the North Men. He fought the battle of Cocboy, in which fell Eawa, son of Pybba, his brother, king of the Mercians, and Oswald, king of the North-men, and he gained the victory by diabolical agency. He was not baptized, and never believed in God.

66. From the beginning of the world to Constantinus and Rufus, are found to be five thousand six hundred and fifty-eight years.

Also from the two consuls, Rufus and Rubelius, to the consul Stilicho, are three hundred and seventy-three years.

Also from Stilicho to Valentinian, son of Placida, and the reign of Vortigern, are twenty-eight years.

And from the reign of Vortigern to the quarrel between Guitolinus and Ambrosius, are twelve years, which is Guoloppum, that is Catgwaloph.* Vortigern reigned in Britain when Theodosius and Valentinian were consuls, and in the fourth year of his reign the Saxons came to Britain, in the consulship of Felix and Taurus, in the four hundredth year from the incarnation of our Lord Jesus Christ.

* In Carmarthenshire. Perhaps the town now called Kidwelly.

From the year in which the Saxons came into Britain, and were received by Vortigern, to the time of Decius and Valerian, are sixty-nine years.

CONTENTS

I. THE PROLOGUE. 3
II. THE APOLOGY OF NENNIUS 5
III. THE HISTORY 6
THE GENEALOGY OF THE KINGS OF BERNICIA.* 48
THE GENEALOGY OF THE KINGS OF KENT. 49
THE ORIGIN OF THE KINGS OF EAST-ANGLIA 49
THE GENEALOGY OF THE MERCIANS. 50
THE KINGS OF THE DEIRI. 50

Milton Keynes UK
Ingram Content Group UK Ltd.
UKHW010226230124
436511UK00003B/137